Muddy-One and Pranky 7

The Gossamer Elf 16

Tammylin's Friend 22

The Tale of Snips 28

The Magic Bubble Pipes 32

The Tale of Jig and Jog 39

The Cat Without Whiskers 45

The Winter Wide-Awakes 53

Enid Blyton's

TELL-A-STORY BOOK

The Gossamer Elf
and other stories

Muddy-One and Pranky

"THERE goes old Muddy-One!" said the big water-snail. "Look out, you young frogs."

The little frogs swam up to the top of the pond at once. They were all afraid of Muddy-One. He was a large, ugly grub who lurked in the mud, and was always hungry.

Curly-Shell, the snail, wasn't at all afraid of Muddy-One. He had only to curl himself up in his hard shell whenever he spied the big grub, and nobody could harm him then. But most of the other creatures in the pond were afraid of the ugly old grub.

Pranky, the water-pixie, teased him dreadfully. He was a naughty little mischief, very quick and cheeky, and the names he called Muddy-One made all the snails and fishes laugh.

Muddy-One had been in the pond for a very long time. He had been small at first, but now he was big. He crawled about in the mud, and across his face he put a curious claw, which could shoot out and catch any little water creature in its pincers.

He didn't like being teased by Pranky. "I can't help being ugly," he would say; "I didn't make myself. If I could have made myself I would have given myself beautiful wings, and a gleaming body, and I wouldn't live down here in the slimy mud, but up in the sunshine. Sometimes I crawl up a water-plant and look out of the water. Up there is a lovely world of light and warmth. I wish I belonged to it."

"Well, you don't! An ugly creature like you wouldn't be allowed to live up in the bright sunshine," said Pranky, and he poked the grub with a bit of stick. "How lazy you are! Stir yourself! Gallop round the pond a bit."

But Muddy-One wasn't very gallopy. He didn't like being poked with a stick, and he was angry with the unkind little pixie. But that only made Pranky call him ruder names than ever; so in the end Muddy-One buried himself deep down in the slime and tried to hide.

"He's ashamed of himself, and I don't wonder," cried Pranky, poking his stick into the mud. "What a pity somebody doesn't eat him. I'll find a big fish one day, Muddy-One, and send him along to eat you."

"You shouldn't tease Muddy-One so," said the big water-snail. "He doesn't do you any harm. You're unkind."

Then Pranky swam to the snail and tried to pull him out of his shell. But he couldn't. So he wrote a rude sentence on the snail's shell and left him. He put "I am a poor old slow-coach," all over the snail's shell, and the snail couldn't think why everyone who met him laughed.

Pranky was just as much at home in the air as in the water. He was a lucky fellow, for he could run

and swim and fly. He was a fine-looking pixie too, and he knew it. He often used a shining dew-drop as a mirror, and looked at himself proudly in it.

One day the Princess Melisande thought she would give a party. Now, she lived high up on a hill above the clouds, so it was plain that every guest would have to fly there.

"I shall get my Peacock butterfly to take me," said Jinky the fairy.

"I'm going on Zoom the bumble-bee," said Tippy the goblin.

"I've got my lovely Tiger-moth," said Twink the elf.

"What are *you* going on, Pranky?" asked Jinky.

"I shall ask the blue-bottle to fly to Princess Melisande's with me," said Pranky. "He's such a lovely colour."

But he couldn't ride the blue-bottle because somebody saw it crawling with dirty feet over a baby's milk-bottle, and the baby's mother killed it.

"He's a dirty, horrid blue-bottle fly," said the mother. "He'll make the baby ill."

9

So there was no blue-bottle for the pixie to ride on. He *was* upset. "Can I ride on Zoom with you?" he asked Tippy.

"No. He says you once sewed up the end of a foxglove flower when he had crawled inside, and he couldn't get out," said Tippy. "He doesn't like you."

"Well, can I come on your butterfly?" Pranky asked Jinky.

"No, you can't. He's isn't strong enough to carry two of us," said Jinky. "Why don't you get a dragon-fly? He'd be very strong indeed, and very beautiful too. He would fly so fast that you'd be at the Princess's in no time!"

"Oooh, yes!—I'd love a dragonfly," said Pranky, thinking how very grand he would feel riding such a lovely creature. "But I haven't seen any yet. Where can I get one?"

"You'd better go and ask old Mother Wimple." said Jinky. "She knows all the insects well. She's always mending their wings for them when they get torn. She could get you a dragonfly, I expect. But be polite to her, Pranky, because she's got a hot temper."

Pranky flew off. He soon came to where Mother Wimple lived. She had a tiny house by the pond, and she was sitting outside it, busily patching the torn wing of a butterfly.

"Mother Wimple, I'm going to Princess Melisande's party," said Pranky, sitting down beside her. "And her palace is so high above the clouds that I've got to get some insect to take me. I want a dragonfly. Could you get me one, please?"

"You're very polite all of a sudden" said old Mother Wimple, who had not heard very good tales of Pranky. "You're one of those people who have very good manners when they want something, and can be very rude when they don't, aren't you?"

"Oh, *no*!" said Pranky, going rather red. "No, I'm very well behaved, Mother Wimple. Please do tell me if you can get me a dragonfly."

"When is the party?" asked Mother Wimple.

"Tomorrow afternoon," said Pranky.

"Come back an hour before you have to set off for the party, and I'll have here the finest dragonfly you ever saw," said Mother Wimple.

Pranky flew off in the greatest delight. He was back in good time the next day, but he couldn't see any dragonfly.

"Be patient," said Mother Wimple. "You'll see him soon. Ah—here he comes."

She pointed to a water-plant whose stem came right up out of the pond. Up it was crawling the ugly old grub, Muddy-One. Pranky stared at him and then he stared at Mother Wimple.

"Why—that's no dragonfly—that's only ugly old Muddy-One!" he said.

"Oh, you know him, do you?" said Mother Wimple. "Well now, you watch and see what is going to happen to him. You'll see something marvellous."

Pranky watched. Muddy-One crawled right out of the water, and clung to the stem of the water-plant, enjoying the hot sunshine.

Then, to the pixie's enormous surprise, the ugly old grub split his skin right down his back!

"Gracious goodness, look at that!" said Pranky. "He's split himself. Has he eaten too much? I always told him he'd burst if he was so greedy."

"Be quiet," said Mother Wimple. "Now look—he's split even farther."

Pranky watched in surprise. He saw that the ugly old grub was trying to creep out of his own skin. How extraordinary!

But what a different creature came out of the old skin! He had a long slender body that gleamed blue green. He had crumpled wings. He had enormous eyes that shone in the sun, and six weak legs that clung to the water-plant for safety.

"Why—Muddy-One's got wings," cried Pranky. "Look—he's spreading them out in the sun to dry them. They are long and lovely, and look at his beautiful blue-green body and eyes. Oh, Mother Wimple, he's not an ugly water-grub any longer, he's a most BEAUTIFUL dragonfly. It's magic, it's magic! Oh, how clever of you to make a dragonfly come out of Muddy's old skin."

"I didn't," said Mother Wimple. "All dragonflies live down in the mud as grubs for a long time. But when the right time comes, they creep up into the

12

sunshine, take off their old skin, and dart up into the air—gay, beautiful dragonflies!"

"Oh, I shall love to ride him," cried Pranky. Mother Wimple called to the dragonfly as he sat sunning his wings.

"Swift-One! Come here and take this pixie to Princess Melisande's."

The drgonfly flew over to Mother Wimple and soared round her head, gleaming in the sun. Pranky stood up in delight.

"Let me ride you, let me ride you!" he cried.

Swift-One the dragonfly flew just out of reach. "What! Let you, a rude and ill-mannered pixie, ride me, the swiftest dragonfly in the world? Certainly not! I haven't forgotten how you teased me and the names you called me, you horrid little pixie!"

"That's not the way to talk, Swift-One," said Mother Wimple sternly. "I have promised Pranky that he shall ride you. Come down, so that he may get on your back."

Swift-One darted down, and Pranky leapt on to his back. The dragonfly soared high in the air at such a pace that Pranky's breath was almost taken away. But then Swift-One began to play tricks.

He stopped suddenly in mid-air, and Pranky almost shot over his head. He flew upside-down, and Pranky nearly fell off. He darted down to the surface of the pond and made the pixie get his feet wet. He teased Pranky just as much as Pranky had once teased him, down in the pond.

Then he turned over and over and over in the air, and at last, the pixie, too giddy to hold on any longer, fell off and flew down to the ground, landing beside Mother Wimple with a bump.

He began to cry when he saw the dragonfly darting away at top speed. Mother Wimple laughed.

"It serves you right," she said. "I thought he would play a few tricks on you if he had the chance. Cry, Pranky, cry! Perhaps you will learn now not to make fun of ugly, slow creatures. You never know when they are going to change into beautiful, swift flying things that will tip you off their backs."

"I c-c-c-can't go to the party now," wept Pranky. "Tippy's gone by on his butterfly, and Jinky's gone on Zoom the bumble-bee, but I've got no one to take *me*!"

He went home, very sorry for himself. And all that August and September he had to keep a sharp look out for Swift-One, because the dragonfly flew down to nip the bad little pixie whenever he saw him.

Have you seen Swift-One, the dragonfly? Look out for him. He's beautiful.

The Gossamer Elf

EVERYBODY knew the Gossamer Elf. She was the cleverest dressmaker in the whole of Fairyland. You should have seen the dresses and cloaks she made!

"I think her autumn clothes are the best," said Winks. "She made me a lovely dress last October of a red creeper leaf. I went to lots of parties in it."

"She made me a cloak out of a pair of beech leaves," said Feefo. "It was a golden cloak, the prettiest I ever had."

"Her stitches are the finest I ever saw," said Tiptoe. "Well—they're so fine I can't see them! Once I thought that the Gossamer Elf didn't sew our frocks at all, but just made them by magic. She doesn't though, I've seen her sewing away with a tiny, tiny needle."

"Ah, but have you seen her thread?" said Winks. "It's so fine and so strong that once she's put a stitch into a frock, it never comes undone."

"What does she use for thread?" said Feefo. "I'd like to get some. I'll go and ask her."

So she went to call on the Gossamer Elf. But the Elf was out. She had left her door open and Feefo went inside. On a shelf she saw reels upon reels—but they were all empty. Not one reel had any thread on it. How strange!

Soon the Gossamer Elf came in. Feefo ran to her.

"I've come to ask you something. Where do you get your fine thread? I can't see any on your reels."

The Gossamer Elf smiled. "No—my reels are all empty now," she said. "But soon they will be filled again with the finest, silkiest thread. I always get my thread at this time of year, you know."

"Where from?" asked Feefo. "Can I get some too? Do let me. Take me with you and I'll buy some."

"I don't buy it," said the Elf. "Yes, you can come with me if you like. I'm starting out tomorrow morning at dawn. You can carry some of my empty reels with you. That will be a help."

So Feefo and the Gossamer Elf set out at dawn. They went to the fields. It was a lovely morning, and the sun shone softly from a blue sky.

"It's gossamer time now," said the Elf. "Did you know that? Soon the air will be full of fine silken threads that will stretch across the fields everywhere. See—you can spy some already, gleaming in the sun."

Feefo looked. Yes—she could see some fine, long threads stretching from the hedge above high up into the air. Soon there would be plenty of them.

"But what are those silky threads?" said Feefo in wonder. "Where do they come from? Who makes them?"

"Climb up the hedge with me and I'll show you," said the Elf. "Some very small friends of mine make them. We'll watch them."

18

They climbed up the hedge together, using the prickles on the wild rose stems as steps. They soon got high up in the hedge. Then Feefo saw around her many tiny spiders—young ones, not much more than babies.

Some stood on leaves, some clung to stems, and all of them were doing the same thing. They were sending out long silken threads from underneath their bodies.

"They have their silk spinnerets there," said the Elf. "Big spiders have too. They take the thread from their spinnerets. Watch that tiny spider. See the long thread coming out, and waving in the air."

"Oh, yes," said Feefo, in surprise. She saw dozens of tiny spiders all doing the same thing. "But why are they all doing this, Elf? It seems very queer to me. They are not spinning webs."

"No, they are going out into the world to seek their fortunes," said the Elf. "Each baby spider wants to leave the place where he was born. He wants to journey far away and find his own place to live. So he is sending out a long, long thread into the air—and then, when he has a long enough line, he will let the wind take him off into the air with his gossamer thread—and, like a tiny parachutist, he will soar over the world, and then drop gently to ground."

"Goodness me!" said Feefo, astonished. "Look, there goes one, Elf! Away he goes on the wind."

The tiny spider had let go his hold of the leaf, and

now, swinging gently on the end of his gossamer thread he let himself be carried away on the breeze, exactly like a tiny parachutist. Feefo and the Elf watched him soaring away, until he could no longer be seen.

"They're all doing it, all the baby spiders!" cried Feefo in delight. "Oh, look at them swinging away on their threads. The wind blows the threads away and the spiders go with them!"

They watched the curious sight for a little while. Then Feefo turned to the Elf. "But Elf," she said, "surely you don't take their threads away from the tiny spiders? That would be a most unkind thing to do."

"Of course I don't," said the Elf. "How could you think I'd do that? No—once the spiders have made their journey and landed safely somewhere, they don't want their threads any more. So I collect them on my reels, you see. I wind them up carefully, and soon have all my reels full for my year's work."

"Well, what a good idea," cried Feefo. "Look— there comes a spider from far away; see him swinging down on the end of his line? Here he is, just beside us. Little spider, what an adventure you've had!"

"May I take your thread please, if you don't want it any more?" asked the Gossamer Elf politely. "Oh, thank you. What a nice long one!"

She began to wind the gossamer round and round her reel. Soon the reel was full. The spider ran off to find himself a nice new home under a leaf. Maybe he would catch plenty of flies there, he thought. Soon he would spin a fine web, and wait for his dinner to come along and fly into it.

Another spider landed a little farther down. Feefo ran to him. As soon as he had cast off his gossamer she began to wind it round and round the reel she carried. "What fun this is!" she thought. "Now I know why the Gossamer Elf has her name. How clever she is to think of this idea!"

Day after day, early in the morning, Feefo and the Gossamer Elf came out together, and waited for the adventuring spiders to land near them on their gossamer lines. Soon they had dozens and dozens of reels full of the fine silken thread.

"There. We've got enough!" said the Elf at last. "Now I shall wait for the leaves to change colour and soon I shall be hard at work again making winter dresses and cloaks and sewing them with the gossamer thread given me by the tiny spiders. I shall be very busy indeed this winter!"

So she is. She is making coats of blackberry leaves, crimson, yellow and pink; frocks of golden hazel leaves, trimmed with berries and cloaks of brilliant cherry leaves. You should see them! But you can't see her stitches—they are made of the gossamer from the spiders.

Have you ever seen it? You really must. You can take some too, if you want, for the spiders won't need it again.

Tammylin's friend

ONCE upon a time there was a little pixie who didn't like earwigs. Now this was very silly because earwigs are clean and tidy creatures and never mind doing a good turn to the fairies.

Still, Tammylin the pixie couldn't bear an earwig near her, and whenever she saw one she always sent it scurrying away in fright. She kept a little broom which she used specially for frightening earwigs, and she often used to sweep away any that came near her neat little house and garden.

Now one day when Tammylin was wandering in the violet wood all by herself, humming a song and dancing round the sweet-smelling violets, she walked quite by mistake into the Green Magician's garden.

He lived in the middle of the wood, and as he had no wall or fence or hedge round his garden it was very difficult to see it. Tammylin didn't see it at all—and she walked right into it just as the Green Magician was coming out to do his shopping!

"Oho!" he said, and caught hold of Tammylin, who was alarmed and astonished. "So you've come spying round, have you, to see what kind of secret magic I make? Well, you'll be sorry now! You can be my cook. The rabbit who waited on me has just left to get married—you will do nicely instead."

"I won't, I won't!" squealed Tammylin, and she wriggled as hard as she could. But it wasn't a bit of good. The Green Magician wrapped her up in his green cloak and took her into his cottage. He cut off her pretty silver wings and gave her an apron to wear.

"My wings won't grow for three weeks," sobbed Tammylin. "You are very horrid. I shall run away as soon as you've gone out."

"Oh, no, you won't!" said the Green Magician— and what do you think he did? Why, he took his magic wand, waved it round his garden seven times and called out a magic word—and lo and behold! a great wall grew round it, so high that Tammylin couldn't see the top.

"There," said the magician, pleased. "What do you think of that? You can't escape now."

He went out to do his shopping, unlocking and locking a big door in the wall. Tammylin was left alone to cook the dinner. How she wished she could let her friends know where she was!

When the Green Magician went to market, he heard everyone talking about Tammylin's dis-appearance, but he didn't say a word. No, he had got a cook for nothing, and he meant to keep her. He went to the fish-stall and bought some herrings. He went to the sweet-stall and bought some pepper-mints. He went to the fruit-stall and there he bought some pears and a large cauliflower.

He carried them all home in his big bag, and went in through the door in the wall again, locking it after him. He put his shopping down on the kitchen table and told Tammylin to cook the cauliflower for dinner.

"I'm going into the garden to water my flowers," he said. So out he went, and left Tammylin to get on with the cooking. The litle pixie sulkily took up the cauliflower—and as she did so out crept a very large earwig. Tammylin dropped the cauliflower with a shriek.

"Hello, Tammylin," said the earwig in surprise. "How did you come to be here?"

"The Green Magician caught me," said Tammylin, "and I can't escape because there's a high wall round the garden and my wings are cut off. Oh, go away, you horrid earwig! If only you were a butterfly you could fly up over the wall and tell everyone where I am. Then my friends would rescue me. What a pity you are such an ugly, useless earwig."

"You are unkind, Tammylin," said the earwig.

Just then the Green Magician poked his head in at the window. "Who are you talking to?" he said.

"To an earwig, the horrid thing!" said Tammylin.

"Oh, an earwig," said the Magician. "Well, *he's* a prisoner here too—he can crawl around the garden but he can't get out. If it had been a butterfly, a bee, or a moth I'd have stopped him from taking any message to your friends. But an earwig has no wings."

As soon as the magician had gone back to the garden the earwig ran close to Tammylin and began to whisper.

"Listen, Tammylin, the magician is wrong," it said. "I *have* got wings."

Tammylin stared in surprise at the brown, smooth-backed earwig. "You haven't!" she said. "What a storyteller you are!"

"Sh!" said the earwig. "I tell you I *have* got wings. I keep them neatly folded under my back-shell. Look, those brown things on my back are my wing-cases. Watch how I unfold my beautiful gauzy

wings."

Tammylin watched in the greatest astonishment. The earwig lifted up his brown wing-cases from his back and shook out his wings. They were gauzy like a bee's, but long and beautifully folded—just like a fan.

The earwig spread them out. "I'm going off to tell your friend where you are," he said. "They will rescue you soon. Good-bye."

Tammylin watched the earwig fly up into the air on his long gauzy wings, up, up and up—right over the wall. The Green Magician never even saw him.

"Well," thought Tammylin, washing the cauli-flower, "I never knew before that earwigs had wings folded so beautifully under their back-shells. How kind of him to fly off to tell my friends. I wish I hadn't been so horrid to earwigs. I never will be

26

again!"

The earwig flew straight to the market-place, folded his wings neatly, poked them tidily under his back-shell with his pincers, and then told everyone where he had seen Tammylin. It wasn't long before the King himself, at the head of twenty men, was riding through the violet wood to rescue Tammylin. But as soon as the Magician heard his King's voice he took down the wall, and fled away to the borders of Fairyland. He knew that it was forbidden to capture pixies.

"But how, how, *how* did the King know where Tammylin was?" he wondered a hundred times a day. He never knew—but Tammylin did not forget her kind friend.

"I will never chase earwigs away again," she said. "I didn't know they were so kind, and had such lovely wings, folded like fans."

"Oh, earwigs are good people," said the King, as she rode back safely with him. "They look after their little ones as few insects do—they are very good mothers. You should not be unkind to anything, Tammylin. Goodness and loveliness may be found in even the ugliest creatures. You never know!"

Now Tammylin is friends with all the earwigs, beetles and spiders that she knows, and never dreams of using her broom to sweep them away. Wasn't it a good thing for her that an earwig had wings! Did *you* know that?

The Tale of Snips

SNIPS was a tailor. He made red and yellow coats, brown tunics and cobweb cloaks for party wear. In the autumn he did a roaring trade, for then there were many bright leaves tumbling down from the trees for him to cut up and make into elfin clothes. He was always very busy then.

One year the King himself ordered twelve coats from Snips, all different colours, and each with a hat made of an acorn-cup to match. It was a busy time for Snips.

He managed to get them all done, and one night he set out with the twelve coats in a big bag. With him he took needle and thread, two thimbles and an extra large packet of pins, besides his best silver scissors. Then, if there were any alterations needed he could do them at once, without taking the coats back again.

The King was delighted with the coats. Not one of them needed to be altered; they all fitted perfectly.

"You're a fine tailor, Snips," said the King to the proud little goblin. "I will pay you tonight. You shall have a piece of gold for each coat. Here you are—twelve golden pounds. Take care of them."

Snips put them into his leather purse, thanked the King and went on his way home, planning all the marvellous things he would do with his money. But there was someone following him—a small green gnome who meant to rob him before he reached home!

Snips didn't know. He went humming along, until he came to the big friendly chestnut tree that

stood in the middle of the wood. And just as he passed under it, the leaves began to whisper to him.

"Snips, Snips, there's a robber behind you! Hide, Snips, hide!"

Snips was frightened almost out of his life. He jumped high into the air, caught hold of a low branch and pulled himself up on it. He sat there trembling. Soon he saw the green gnome passing silently underneath, never guessing that Snips was hidden above him.

"Let me stay hidden in your leaves for the night," begged Snips. "In the morning light I can go home safely with my money."

So he stayed there in safety all the night long. In the morning he asked the chestnut tree what he could do in return for its help.

"I suppose you couldn't stop the horses and donkeys eating my chestnuts when they fall to the ground, could you?" asked the tree. "It's such a nuisance."

Snips picked from the tree a round, smooth case, inside which lay two brown, polished chesnuts. "Of course I can help you!" he cried. "I'll stick heaps of pins into the cases, head downwards, with their points outwards. Then no animal will like to eat them."

And that is just what he did. The next year the pins grew from the chestnut cases, and ever since then they have been as prickly as can be. Feel them and see!

The Magic Bubble Pipes

MERRY and Bright were hard at work making their famous bubble pipes. They were pretty little pipes, carved neatly round the bowl, and the brownies sold them for a penny each. Merry and Bright sold hundreds of them, for the fairies loved to blow bubbles. Sometimes the little folk sailed off on a big one, and sometimes they took their little scissors and snipped pieces off the brightest coloured bubbles to make into frocks and coats.

Now one day Dame Tiptap came along and looked at the little pipes. She didn't want to buy one, but she liked to watch the two brownies making them.

Merry and Bright thought she was a funny old dame.

"Do you want a pipe to smoke, Dame Tiptap?" asked Merry.

"Of course not," said the old lady angrily. "You know I would never dream of smoking a pipe. Don't be rude!"

"Have a look at this one, Dame Tiptap," said Bright, and he held up a long-stemmed pipe to the old dame. It was filled with soapy water, but Dame Tiptap didn't know that. She put on her glasses to have a look, for she thought the pipe must be a special one.

JOYCE JOHNSON

"Smell it," said Bright, with a giggle. Dame Tiptap bent closer and smelt it, and at that very moment Bright blew hard down the stem of the pipe, and some soapy bubbles rose out of the bowl and burst in the old dame's face. What a fright she got! She nearly fell over, and how those two rascally brownies roared to see her face all over bubbles.

"That is very rude and unkind of you," said Dame Tiptap angrily. "You deserve to be punished for that." She took out a yellow box, and from it scattered a misty powder over the brownies' hands.

"There's a spell in that," she said, "and it's gone into your fingers now. Whatever you make will get a bit of the spell, when the powder works. Ha, ha, Merry and Bright, you'll soon wish you hadn't played a trick on old Tiptap!"

Off she went, wiping her soapy face. The brownies looked at one another in dismay, and then looked at their hands. They seemed all right. Whatever could the spell be?

"Oh, it's just nothing," said Merry at last. "She was trying to frighten us, that's all. Silly old dame."

They went on with their work, and made dozens of bubble pipes that day, but the spell went into many of the pipes as they worked, and lay there until the right time came.

Twelve of the pipes had the spell. The rest were all right. The little folk came to buy the pipes, and took them home. They made soapy water and put the pipes to their mouths, and blew bubbles.

And then those pipes that had the spell in them began to act very queerly indeed! Even when the fairy stopped blowing, the soapy bubbles went on coming out of the pipe! Soon the room was full of bubbles, but still the pipe went on blowing them out. They floated out of the window. They floated through the wood, and then, one by one, they burst.

And, dear me, each bubble burst with a bang as loud as a gun going off. It made everyone jump nearly out of their skins, and the King cried: "Guns! Is that an enemy coming?"

Bang! Bang! Bang! The bubbles went on bursting as they flew out of the pipes. The King and his courtiers sent orders to the army to turn out. It must be an enemy coming! Bang! BANG!

The army turned out, and aeroplanes buzzed over-head to see if they could find the enemy with so many guns. But not a sign of anyone could they see. Just then some of the bubbles, which had floated high in the air, burst near the aeroplanes. Bang! Bang! Pop! Bang!

"We are being shot at!" cried the airmen, and raced downwards to tell the King. What a to-do there was! All that day, as the bubbles popped and banged messengers rushed here and there trying to find out what was the matter, and the army marched north, south, east and west to stop the enemy that nobody could see.

And then at last bubbles floated into the palace garden, and the King saw what he had thought was the banging of guns was really the popping of magic bubbles. How annoyed he was. To think he had called out his army and his air force to fight a lot of bubbles!

It wasn't long before he had Merry and Bright before him and was asking them the meaning of such a thing. They were trembling, because they had not known that the spell would cause the pipes to go on pouring out bubbles without a stop, bubbles that banged like guns when they burst.

They told the King everything, and he sent for Dame Tiptap too. Merry and Bright felt ashamed of themselves when the old dame told of the trick they had played on her.

"You should not have blown such a powerful spell over their hands," said the King. "It has caused a great deal of trouble. Take the spell off their hands, Dame Tiptap."

"I can't, Your Majesty," said the old lady. "It is there for good."

"Well, they will have to put up with it, then," said the King. "But I doubt if anyone will buy their pipes now that they know what dreadful bubbles they blow. Take the magic pipes, Dame Tiptap, and destroy them. We cannot have them pouring out bubbles like this."

So the pipes were burnt, and the bang-bang-bang of bursting bubbles stopped. There was peace once more.

But Merry and Bright found that the King was

right when he said that no one would want to buy their pipes any more. Everyone was too much afraid of getting an enchanted pipe. They didn't want that! So they went to the yellow goblin, who also sold pipes, and bought them from him, and Merry and Bright found that they were getting very poor indeed.

"What shall we do?" said Merry. But Bright didn't know. The two brownies could not do anything else but make pipes. They sat and looked as miserable as could be.

And then an old oak tree near by spoke to them.

"I will buy your pipes to put my acorns in," said the tree. "But as I have about a thousand acorns this year, I cannot pay you a penny for each of your pipes. I shall give you one penny for a hundred pipes. That's all."

"But we should have to work dreadfully, dreadfully hard then!" cried Merry.

"Hard work never hurt anyone," said the oak tree. "Well, take it or leave it. You'll find no one else buys your pipes now, and it surely is better to sell them at a penny a hundred than to have them falling to bits in your cupboard!"

Well, there was some sense in what the tree said, and the two brownies had to agree. But how hard they had to work now—and for such a little money too! They made the little pipes all day long, and at night they set the acorns neatly into them, so that each acorn had a little resting-place and did not easily fall of the tree when the wind blew. The oak tree made them carve the pipes neatly, just as before.

Merry and Bright are not quite so merry and bright now! But still, as the oak tree said, hard work never hurt anyone; and although the two brownies haven't nearly so much money as they used to have, they still have time to play now and again. You will usually see them in an oak wood, hard at work on their tiny pipes; and it is said that some of the pipes have that magic spell in them still, so if you want a bit of excitement, try blowing bubbles through a few of the acorn pipes and see if anything happens. You never know!

And don't forget to see how neatly Merry and Bright carve the bowls of their pipes, and how beautifully they make them to fit each acorn.

The Tale of Jig and Jog

ONE day Jig and Jog, the two brownies who lived in Hollyhock Cottage, made up their minds to give a party.

"It shall be a birthday party," said Jig. "Then everyone will bring us presents. Won't that be nice, Jog?"

"Rather!" said Jog, rubbing his horny little hands in glee. "Ha! Presents of cakes! And sweets! And all kinds of exciting things!"

"We will give our party on November the fourteenth," said Jig. "We will send out the invitation cards now."

"Who shall come to the party?" said Jog.

"Well, we will ask Prickles the hedgehog," said Jig. "He makes beautiful cakes. He might bring us one. We will put on our invitation cards that it is a birthday party. Then he will know he must bring a present."

"Who else shall come?" asked Jog.

"Well, Slinky the snake would be a good person to ask," said Jig, "and so would Slow-One the toad; and his cousin, Hoppity, the frog. Oh, and don't you think we could ask that bird who plays hide-and-seek so well—what's his name, now?"

"You mean the cuckoo," said Jog. "Yes, we will ask him too; and we will ask Dozy the little dormouse, for he is a generous fellow, and might even bring us a present each, instead of one between us."

The two brownies made out their list and then wrote out their invitation cards.

"Please come to a birthday party at Hollyhock Cottage on November the fourteenth, at four o'clock." they wrote on each card. Then they posted all the cards in the pillar-box at the end of the road, and waited for the answers.

The postman, Floppy the rabbit, took the cards and went to deliver them. He knew where Prickles the hedgehog lived, in a cosy hole in the sunny bankside of the hedge. He slipped the card into the hole. He knew where Slinky the snake lived too—in the old hollow tree in the middle of the wood. He climbed up and dropped the card down into the hole. He was a very good postman.

Then Floppy took Slow-One's card, and went to a big stone by the pond. He knew Slow-One the toad lived there. He pushed the card under the stone and left it. Hoppity the frog lived in the pond. Floppy waited until a stickleback came up to the top of the water and asked him to take the card to Hoppity. The fish caught the card neatly in its mouth and swam off with it.

"Now there's the card for the cuckoo," said Floppy Rabbit to himself. "Well, he was always sitting in that big beech tree, calling Cuckoo to everyone, so I'll put his card there. He is sure to see it if he sits there again."

Floppy had only one card left now—and that was for Dozy the dormouse. Floppy knew quite well where Dozy was living. He was in a cosy hole deep down in the roots of the big fir tree at the edge of the wood, not far from Floppy's own burrow. So, being a sensible rabbit, Floppy left that card till last, stuffed it into Dozy's hole, and then slipped into his own burrow for a rest and a cup of carrot tea.

Jig and Jog waited impatiently for the answers to

their invitations. But none came! It was most extraordinary. Jig and Jog were puzzled. And then Jig thought he knew why. They had not put on the cards that they wanted an answer! So perhaps all their guests had thought they need not reply. Well, it didn't matter. The two brownies felt quite sure they would all turn up at the party on the right day—each bringing a very nice present!

They began to get ready for the party. They each had a new suit made, a red one for Jig and a blue one for Jog. They made a batch of chocolate cakes and a batch of ginger ones. They made strawberry jam sandwiches. They put out a clean cloth and arranged chairs all round their small table.

"We said four o'clock on the invitation cards," said Jig, when the day came. "It's half-past three now. Are we quite, quite ready, Jog?"

"Well, we've put on our new suits, and we've laid the table and put out the cakes and sandwiches and arranged the chairs," said Jog. "Yes, we are quite ready. I wonder who will come first!"

"And I wonder what everyone will bring us," said Jig. "It's a good thing we told everyone it was a birthday party, so that we can get presents."

Four o'clock came—but nobody walked up the garden path. How strange! Quarter-past four and still no guests! Half-past four—five o'clock! Where could everyone be? There were the cakes and the sandwiches—but no guests to eat them. Jig and Jog looked as if they were going to cry!

They went down the garden path and looked up and down the road. Only Dame Chippy was there coming along with the washing. When she saw their sad faces she stopped.

"What's the matter?" she asked.

"Well," said Jig mournfully, "we sent out invitations to Prickles, Slinky, Slow-One, Hoppity, the cuckoo and Dozy to come to a birthday party today—and nobody's come—and we shan't get any presents."

"Don't you know that you never tell anyone a party is a *birthday* party?" said Dame Chippy, shocked. "Why, that's just asking for presents, and nobody with good manners does that. It serves you right that nobody has come."

"But *why* haven't they come?" wailed Jog.

"If you think hard you'll know," said Dame Chippy, with a grin.

Jig and Jog thought hard—but they didn't know. Do you? Dame Chippy had to tell them.

"You are two silly creatures," she said. "Don't you know that Prickles the hedgehog always finds a hole for himself in the winter and sleeps the cold days away? Don't you know that Slinky the snake hates the cold and hides in a hollow tree fast asleep until the spring comes? And Slow-One the toad is never awake in the winter, sillies! He is sound asleep under his big stone—and his cousin, Hoppity the frog, is hidden in the mud at the bottom of the pond! As for the cuckoo, he has left the land months ago. He always goes south for the winter to find warmth and food."

"What about Dozy?" asked Jig in a small voice.

"He sleeps more soundly than any of them!" said Dame Chippy. "He's snoring in the roots of the old fir tree! Well, well, well—no wonder you have no guests and no birthday presents! It serves you right for being so stupid and greedy!"

"Oh, all our cards were wasted, and all our cakes will be wasted too," wept Jig and Jog in dismay.

"Your cakes needn't be wasted!" said Dame Chippy. "I'll come in and eat them for you!"

And so she did—but Jig and Jog weren't a bit pleased. What sillies they were, weren't they?

The Cat Without Whiskers

INKY was a black cat, with the finest white whiskers in the street. He was a handsome cat, with sharp ears and a long thick tail that looked like a snake when he waved it to and fro. He had a white mark under his chin which the children called his feeder, and he washed it three times a day, so that it was always like snow.

Inky was plump, for he was the best ratter and mouser in the town, and never lacked a good dinner. When he sat on the wall washing himself he was a fine sight, for his glossy fur gleamed in the sun and his whiskers stuck out each side of his face like white wires.

"I'm the finest-looking cat in the town," said Inky proudly, and he looked scornfully down at the tabby in the garden below, and the white cat washing itself on a window-sill near by. "Nobody is so good-looking as me!"

Then there came by a little boy, and when he saw the big black cat sitting up on the wall, he shouted up at him, laughing, "Hallo, Whiskers!"

Inky was offended. His name wasn't Whiskers. It was Inky. A little girl heard what the boy said and she laughed. "That's a good name for him," she said. "He's a very whiskery cat. Whiskers! Whiskers!"

Everyone thought it a funny name, and soon Inky was being called Whiskers all day long, even by the cats and dogs around. This made him really very angry.

"It's a horrid, silly name," he thought crossly, "and it's rude of people to call me that. They don't call that nice old gentleman with the beard 'Whiskers', do they? And they don't shout 'Nosy' at that boy with the big nose. I shan't answer them when they call me Whiskers!"

So he didn't—but it wasn't any good, for everyone shouted "Whiskers! Whiskers!" as soon as they saw Inky's wonderful whiskers.

Inky thought hard. "I shall get rid of my whiskers," he said to himself. "Yes—I shall start a new fashion for cats. We won't have whiskers. After all, men shave every morning, and people think that is a good idea. I will shave my whiskers off, and then no one will call me Whiskers."

He told his idea to wise old Shellyback the tortoise. Shellyback listened and pulled at the grass he was eating.

"It is best not to meddle with things you have been given," he said. "You will be sorry."

"No, I shan't," said Inky. "My whiskers are no

use to me that I can see—I shall shave them off!"

Well, he slipped into the bathroom at his home early the next morning and found the thing his master called a razor. In a trice Inky had shaved his beautiful whiskers off. They were gone. He was no longer a whiskery cat.

He looked at himself in the glass. He did look a bit queer—but at any rate no one would now shout Whiskers after him. He slipped down the stairs and out into the garden. He jumped on the wall in the sun.

The milkman came by and looked at him. He did not shout "Whiskers!" as he usually did. He stared in rather a puzzled way and said nothing at all. Then a little boy came by delivering papers, and he didn't shout "Whiskers!" either.

Inky was pleased. At last he had got rid of his horrid name. He sat in the sun, purring, and soon his friends gathered round him. There was Tabby from next door, the white cat Snowball, Shellyback the tortoise, who looked up at him from the lawn, and the old dog Rover, who never chased cats.

"What's the matter with you this morning, Inky?" asked Snowball, puzzled. "You look different."

"His whiskers are gone," said Tabby, startled. "How strange."

"How did you lose them?" asked Rover.

"I shaved them off," said Inky proudly. "I am starting a new fashion for cats. Grown-up men shave their whiskers off each day, don't they? Well, why should cats have whiskers? Don't you think I look much smarter now?"

Everyone stared at Inky, but nobody said a word. They all thought Inky looked dreadful without his whiskers.

"You'll soon see every animal following my fashion of no whiskers," said Inky. "It's so much

more comfortable. Whiskers always get in my way when I'm washing my face, but now I can wash it as smoothly as anything. Look!"

He washed his face with his paw. Certainly it

looked easier to do it without whiskers. But the older animals shook their heads.

"Whiskers are some use or we wouldn't have them," said Tabby.

"Well, what use *are* they?" said Inky.

But nobody was clever enough to think of anything to say in answer to that. One by one they slipped off to their homes to dinner, quite determined that *they* were not going to shave off their whiskers, whatever Inky did.

Now that night Inky felt very hungry. He had been late for tea that afternoon and a stray dog had gone into his garden and eaten up the plate of fish and milk that his mistress had put out for him. Inky was annoyed.

"Never mind," he thought to himself. "I'll go hunting tonight. I'll catch a few mice and perhaps a rat or two. I know a good place in the hedge at the bottom of the garden. I'll hide on one side of it and wait for the night animals to come out."

So off he went when darkness came and crouched down on one side of the hedge. Soon he heard the pitter-pattering of little mice-feet. Inky stiffened and kept quite still. In a moment he would squeeze through the hedge and pounce on those foolish mice.

He took a step forward. His paw was like velvet and made no noise. He pushed his head into a hole in the hedge—then his body—but alas for Inky! His body was too big for the hole, and the hedge creaked as he tried to get through. The mice heard the noise and shot off into their holes. Not one was left.

"Bother!" said Inky crossly. "I'll wait again. I believe that old rat has a run here somewhere. I'd like to catch him!"

So he waited—and sure enough the big rat ran silently by the hedge. Inky heard him and began to creep towards him; but his fat body brushed against some leaves and the rat heard and fled.

Inky was astonished. Usually he could hunt marvellously with a single sound. Why was it that his body seemed so clumsy tonight? Why did he brush against things and make rustling noises? It was most annoying.

And then suddenly he knew the reason why. Although he hadn't thought about it, his fine whiskers had always helped him to hunt. They had stretched out each side of his face, and were just about the width of his body. He had known that if he could get his head and whiskers through a hole without touching anything, his body would go through easily too, without a sound.

"It was my whiskers that helped my body to know if it could go easily and silently through the holes and between leaves," thought Inky in despair. "Of course! Why didn't I think of that before? They were just the right width for my body, and I knew quite well if I touched anything with my whiskers that my body would also touch it and make a noise—and so I would go another way!"

Inky was quite right. His whiskers had helped him in his hunting. Now he would not be able to hunt well, for he would never know if his body could squeeze through gaps and holes. He would always be making rustling, crackling noises with leaves and twigs. He would never catch anything. Poor Inky!

You can guess that Inky was always waiting for his mistress to put out his dinner after that—for he hardly ever caught a mouse or rat now. He grew much thinner, and he hid himself away, for he was ashamed to think that he had shaved off the things that had been so useful to him.

"A new fashion indeed!" thought Inky. "I was mad! If only I had my lovely whiskers again I wouldn't mind being called 'Whiskers' a hundred times a day. My life is spoilt. I shall never be able to hunt again."

He was a sad and unhappy cat, ashamed to talk to anyone except wise old Shellyback the tortoise. One day he told Shellyback why he was unhappy. Shellyback looked at him closely and laughed.

"Go and sit up on the wall in the sun and see what happens," he said to Inky. "You'll find your troubles are not so big as you thought they were."

In surprise Inky jumped up on the wall and sat there in the sun. The milkman came by with his cart. He looked up.

"Hallo, Whiskers!" he shouted. "Good old Whiskers!

Inky nearly fell off the wall in astonishment. What! He was called Whiskers again even if he had shaved them off? But silly old Inky had quite forgotten something. What had he forgotten?

He had forgotten that whiskers grow again like hair. His whiskers had grown out fine and long and strong and white—and he had been so miserable that he hadn't even noticed. Silly old Whiskers!

He *was* happy when he found that he had them again. He sat and purred so loudly that Shellyback really thought there was an aeroplane flying somewhere near! It sounded just like it.

And now Inky can hunt again, and is the best mouser in the town. He has grown plump and handsome, and his whiskers are finer than ever. He loves to hear himself called "Whiskers" now. So if you see him up on the wall, black and shining, don't say "Hallo, Inky!"—shout "Good old Whiskers!" and he'll purr like a kettle on the boil!

The Winter Wide-Awakes

MOTHER put her head in at the nursery door and saw a very cosy scene. There was a big fire burning, and three children were sitting by it. Two were playing a game of snap, and the other was reading.

"Do you know who's here?" she said. "Auntie Lou."

"Oh!" said all three children, raising their heads. They were Tessie, Pat and Johnny. Tessie looked a little doubtful.

"I hope she hasn't come to take us for a walk," she said. "Auntie Lou is lovely to go for walks with in the summer, but it's all snowy outside now and very cold. I don't think I want to go out today."

Another head came round the door. It belonged to Auntie Lou. She was dressed in warm tweeds, and had a bright red scarf round her neck. Her head was bare, and her cheeks were as red as her scarf. Her blue eyes twinkled.

"What's this I hear? You don't want to go out with me? Well, I like that! Who came and begged to go out with me every week in the summer? Who went to find conkers and nuts and blackberries with me in the autumn because I knew all the best places?"

"We did," said Pat with a grin. "But, Auntie Lou, we're so warm and cosy here; and there's nothing to see in the country now. Honestly there isn't."

"There's nothing but snow," said Johnny, "and all the birds are gone, and all the animals are asleep."

"What a poor little ignorant boy!" said Auntie Lou, making a funny face. "It's true we shouldn't see anything of the winter sleepers—they're all tucked away in their holes—but we could see plenty of wide-awakes."

"Who are they?" asked Johnny.

"Well, as I came over the fields this morning to pay a call on three lazy children, I saw a beautiful red fox," said Aunie Lou. "He wasn't asleep. He almost bumped into me coming round the hedge. I didn't hear him and I suppose he didn't hear me."

"Oh, a fox!" said Pat. "I'd like to have seen that. Auntie, I'll come with you if you'll show me all the wide-awakes."

"We'll all come," said Tessie, shutting her book. "I'd like to find some wide-awakes too, and some birds as well. Lots have gone away, but we've still plenty left, haven't we, Auntie?"

"Plenty," said her aunt. "Hurry up, then. I'll give you three minutes to put on boots and coats."

They were all ready quickly, for they knew perfectly well that Auntie Lou wouldn't wait for anyone who wasn't. They set off down the snowy garden path.

"You can see how many birds have been in your garden this morning." said Auntie Lou, pointing to some bird-tracks in the snow. "Look, that's where the sparrows have been. See the little footmarks all set out in pairs? That's because they hop with their feet together. And there are the marks of a running bird—his footmarks are behind one another."

Johnny hopped with his feet together, and then ran. He saw that he had left his first footmarks in pairs, but the other marks were spread out behind one another. Auntie Lou laughed. "The footmarks of the Johnny-Bird," she said.

By the frozen pond they came to other bird-prints, and Tessie pointed to them. "Ducks," she said. "You can see the marks of the webbing between their toes."

"Yes. The poor things thought they might have a swim on the pond, and came waddling up from the farm to see," said Auntie Lou. "I wonder what they think when they find they can't splash in the ice."

They left the pond behind and struck across the fields. How lovely they were, all blanketed in snow! The hedges were sprinkled with snow too, but here and there the red hips showed the green, unripe ivy-berries.

"Look, Auntie," said Pat, pointing to some bark in the hedgerow which had been gnawed white. "Who's been doing that? Somebody must have been very hungry to eat bark."

"One of the most wide-awakes," said Auntie Lou. She pointed to some tracks. "Look, rabbit footmarks. The bunnies have been gnawing bark because they are so hungry."

"But why don't they eat the grass?" said Tessie.

The two boys laughed at her.

"How can they when it's deep down under the snow?" said Pat scornfully. "Use your brains, Tessie!"

"Oh, I never thought of that," said Tessie. "Poor little rabbits—they must get awfully hungry when their grass is hidden away. No wonder they come and gnaw at the bark."

"Yes, and the fox knows they will come out to feed somewhere," said Auntie Lou. "So he comes out too, and pads along quietly in the snow, watching for an unwary rabbit. I saw a sad little scattering of grey fur this morning as I came along, to show me where the fox had made his breakfast."

"Look, what's that?" suddenly whispered Johnny, clutching at his aunt's arm. She looked where he was pointing.

"A stoat," she said. "He's after the rabbits, I expect."

"But he's white," said Johnny, amazed. "He wasn't white when we saw him in the summer."

"Ah, he's clever. He changed his dark coat for a white one in the winter when the snow came," said his aunt; "all but the tip of his tail, which is black. Now his enemies can't see him against the white snow."

"Isn't he clever?" said Pat. "He's cleverer than the fox. *He* doesn't change his red coat to white. Does the stoat always change his coat, Auntie Lou?"

56

"Only in cold climates," said his aunt, "not down in the south where it is warmer and there is little snow in the winter. Now look, what's that?"

"A weasel," said Pat. "He's wide awake too, isn't he? Look at him, going along almost like a slinky snake. He's a fierce, lively little fellow."

They went by another farm. The farmer was standing at the door of his cow-shed and hailed them.

"Good-morning. It's a fine morning for a walk, isn't it? It's a pity I can't send my cows out for a walk too. They're tired of standing in their sheds."

"Farmer Toms, have you lots of mice and rats about?" asked Johnny. "We're out looking for wide-awake creatures today, and we've seen plenty; but we've seen no rats nor mice."

"Ah, I've too many—far too many," said the farmer. "Up in the loft there, where I store my grain, I get no end of the creatures. You go up and maybe you'll see some."

They all climbed the ladder and went into the dark loft. They sat down on sacks and kept quiet. Almost at once they heard a squeaking. Then two mice appeared from a hole and scampered over to a bin.

"There are two," called Tessie, but her voice frightened them of course, and they turned to run away; then a rat suddenly appeared and made a dart at one of the mice. Tessie gave a squeal.

"Oh! A rat! Horrid, sharp-nosed thing! Auntie, I

don't like rats. Let's go down."

The mice disappeared, and the rat slunk away too. He was a thin rat and looked very hungry. Perhaps he wasn't very clever at catching mice. Nobody liked the look of him.

"The rat is every animal's enemy, and ours as well," said Auntie Lou. "I haven't anything good to say of him. We should get rid of him in every way we can."

The mice squealed behind the boards. "They are saying 'Hear, hear,'" said Pat, and that made everyone laugh.

They went down the ladder, and told Farmer Toms what they had seen. Then they went into the shed. The cows smelt nice, and turned their big heads to look at the children.

"Where are your sheep?" asked Johnny.

The farmer waved his hand up to the hills. "Away up there in the snow with the shepherd," he said. "He's got them safe, and is expecting their little lambs soon. They're often born in the snowy weather, and they're none the worse for it. You must go and see them when they are born."

The children left the farm and went on their way.

"I wouldn't have believed there was so much to see on a snowy wintry day," said Tessie. "I really wouldn't. Why, it's as interesting as summer-time."

"Look, there's a thrush—and a blackbird too— eating the hips in the snowy hedge," said Pat. "Aren't they enjoying themselves? What a good thing there are berries to feed the hungry birds in the winter!"

"And look at all those chaffinches," said Tessie, as a flock of the bright little birds flew over her head towards the farm. "I've never seen so many chaffinches together before."

"No, in the spring and summer they go about in pairs," said her aunt. "But many birds in winter like to flock together. They are probably going to see if there is any grain round about the farm for them to peck up. Look up into the sky—you'll see some other birds there that flock by the thousand."

"Peewits!" said Johnny. "Don't their wings twinkle as they fly? I do love their call too—just like their name!"

"I should think we've seen all the winter wide-awakes there are now," said Tessie. But Auntie Lou shook her head.

"No, there's another. I saw him this morning as I came through the hazel wood. He *has* been asleep, but this lovely sunny day woke him up. He doesn't mind the snow a bit. Look, there he is, the pretty thing!"

A squirrel suddenly bounded down a tree-trunk and ran right over to the children. Auntie Lou put her hand in her pocket and took out a few shelled nuts. "Here you are," she said to the amusing little squirrel. "I've shelled them for you, so you won't have any bother today."

The squirrel took a nut from her fingers, skipped

away a few paces, then sat up with the nut in his paws and began to eat it quickly. The children watched "Peewits!" said Johnny. "Don't their wings twinklehim in delight.

"He's a great friend of mine," said Auntie Lou. "If he's awake and I walk through his wood, he always comes along to me to see if I've anything for him. I expect he has plenty of nuts and acorns hidden away, but he does love a peanut or brazil nut all ready shelled for him—it makes a change from his own nuts."

"Let's take him home! Oh, do let's take him home!" said Johnny, and he tried to catch the bushy-tailed squirrel; but in a trice the little creature ran up a nearby trunk, his tail out behind him, and sat high above their heads, making a little chattering noise.

"His home is up in that tree," said Auntie Lou. "I've no doubt he has a very cosy hole there, safe from little boys who want to take him home with them."

"Oh, I do like him," said Johnny. "Perhaps in the spring, when he has tiny young squirrel children I could have one of those. I'd love a squirrel-pet. I'd call him Scamper."

The squirrel disappeared into his home. Auntie Lou began to walk through the trees. "It's time we went home too," she said. "Look how the sun is sinking. It will soon be getting dark. Come along."

They ran after her, looking about for more squirrels, but they saw none. Johnny made up his

mind to go to the woods the very next day and make friends with the little squirrel all by himself.

"He's the nicest winter wide-awake we've seen," he said. "What a lot we've met today, Auntie! I'd no idea there were so many birds and animals to see on such a wintry day."

It began to get dark. "We shan't see any more now," said Tessie. But they did! As they walked down the lane home, a little bird kept pace with them, flying from tree to tree as they went, giving them little bursts of song.

"It's a robin," said Auntie Lou. "He is always the latest bird abed. Maybe he's the one that belongs to your garden, children. Look out for him tomorrow, and scatter some crumbs for him."

"We will," said Tessie, opening the garden gate. The robin flew in before her. "Yes, he must be ours. He has come to welcome us home. Auntie, you're coming in to tea, aren't you?"

"Of course," said Auntie Lou. "I think I deserve a very nice tea, with hot scones and home-made jam, after taking you three children out to see so many wide-awakes."

"You do! You do!" chorused the children. And she did, didn't she? I hope you'll see a lot of wide-awakes if *you* go out on a winter's day.

61